Freddy the Frogcaster™ and the Terrible Tornado

With love
Janice Dean
xoxo

By JANICE DEAN "The Weather Machine"

Illustrated by RUSS COX

Freddy the Frogcaster™ and Regnery Kids™ are trademarks of Salem Communications Holding Corporation; Regnery® is a registered trademark of Salem Communications Holding Corporation

Weather-Ready Nation Ambassador™ and the Weather-Ready Nation Ambassador™ logo are trademarks of the U.S. Department of Commerce, National Oceanic and Atmospheric Administration, used with permission.

Cataloging-in-Publication data on file with the Library of Congress

ISBN 978-1-62157-469-9

Published in the United States by
Regnery Kids
An imprint of Regnery Publishing
A Division of Salem Media Group
300 New Jersey Avenue NW
Washington, DC 20001
www.RegneryKids.com

Manufactured in the United States of America

10 9 8 7 6 5 4 3 2 1

Books are available in quantity for promotional or premium use. For information on discounts and terms, please visit our website: www.Regnery.com.

Distributed to the trade by
Perseus Distribution
250 West 57th Street
New York, NY 10107

To Matthew and Theodore, your smiles could
chase away the darkest of storm clouds.

Freddy the Frogcaster is your Weather-Ready Nation Ambassador™,
a program of the National Oceanic and Atmospheric Administration (NOAA)

Freddy the Frogcaster was back at the Frog News Network, keeping an eye on the sky and rehearsing his weather reporting in front of the camera. Fellow frogcasters Sally Croaker and Polly Woggins encouraged Freddy to practice, practice, practice.

So every weekend he would head to the TV station, stand up straight, clear his throat, and deliver the weather on camera.

Spring was an exciting time to watch the sky. The changing seasons can bring all sorts of weather. When you have cold air clashing with the warmth of the daytime sun, the atmosphere can stir up some big thunderstorms, with hail, damaging winds, and even—TORNADOES!

As Freddy looked at his weather charts and forecasting tools like radar and satellite imagery, he realized that Lilypad was in for some pretty dangerous weather.

"Sally," Freddy said, "take a look at this cold front that's coming our way. Today and tomorrow are going to be sunny and warm. But once that cold air pushes in, we could have some big thunderstorms. It looks like we're going to get lots of rain, strong winds, maybe hail, and possibly—"

"TORNADOES!" Polly exclaimed. "Maybe that storm chaser Tad Polar will come to Lilypad. You've heard of him, right, Freddy?"

Oh yes! Freddy had heard of Tad Polar the storm-chasing expert. If there was a tornado nearby, Tad Polar was on the scene, taking pictures and reporting from the touchdown area.

That night, Sally started her frogcast with a Frog News Alert: "Good evening, everyone. I'm Sally Croaker from the Frog News Weather Center. Our storm team has been studying the weather maps, and it looks like we could have some severe storms headed our way.

"Everyone should be prepared for the risk of strong thunderstorms. Some could bring lightning, heavy rain, hailstones, strong winds, and even tornadoes. Please know where to go if there's a tornado watch or warning in your area."

Frog News Alert..... Tornado

Watch Possible..... Frog News

Just then, a large armored vehicle pulled up to the Frog News Network. Freddy looked out the window and saw the famous Tad Polar getting out of his storm truck. Everyone hopped out to greet Tad.

"I hear there's a chance of twisters in this area,"
Tad announced. "Thought I'd swing by and have a
look. Hey, I've got room for one more, anyone want
to come?"

"I'll come!" Freddy exclaimed. "Just don't forget
your emergency kit." Freddy was excited to go storm
chasing. But was he really ready for a tornado?

Freddy hurried home to ask his parents for permission to go. They were busy preparing for the storm. Their emergency kit was stocked, and their weather radio had new batteries so they could listen to the latest storm reports. "Mom, Dad, may I go storm chasing with Tad Polar tomorrow to see if we can spot tornadoes?" Freddy asked.

"That sounds scary," his mother replied. "You of all frogs should know you need to be inside in a safe place if there's a twister nearby."

"Tad is very careful when it comes to dangerous weather, Mom."

Freddy's parents weren't sure this was a good idea, but he convinced them he would be safe.

Freddy met Tad in front of the TV station. "Look, Freddy, the National Weather Service has put a tornado watch out for our area, which means weather conditions are ripe for twisters." They drove around, watching the radar and the dark skies through their windshield.

The wind and rain began to pick up. "Look over there!" Tad shouted. "That's a cumulonimbus cloud. And there's a funnel touching the ground. Holy croaks, folks, that's a tornado!"

"Tad, we need to call the station and give them a report, NOW," said Freddy.

Freddy called in and reported: "Sally, we've got a tornado on the ground. It's in front of us and we are keeping our distance. Every frog in Lilypad needs to take shelter right now! Go to the safest place in

your home. That means your basement if you have one. If not, go to an interior room like a closet or bathroom and stay away from the windows. Do NOT go outside!"

Hunkered down inside the Tadmobile, they could hear emergency sirens going off, warning Lilypad of the approaching tornado. Freddy was nervous. They were a little too close to this terrible tornado!

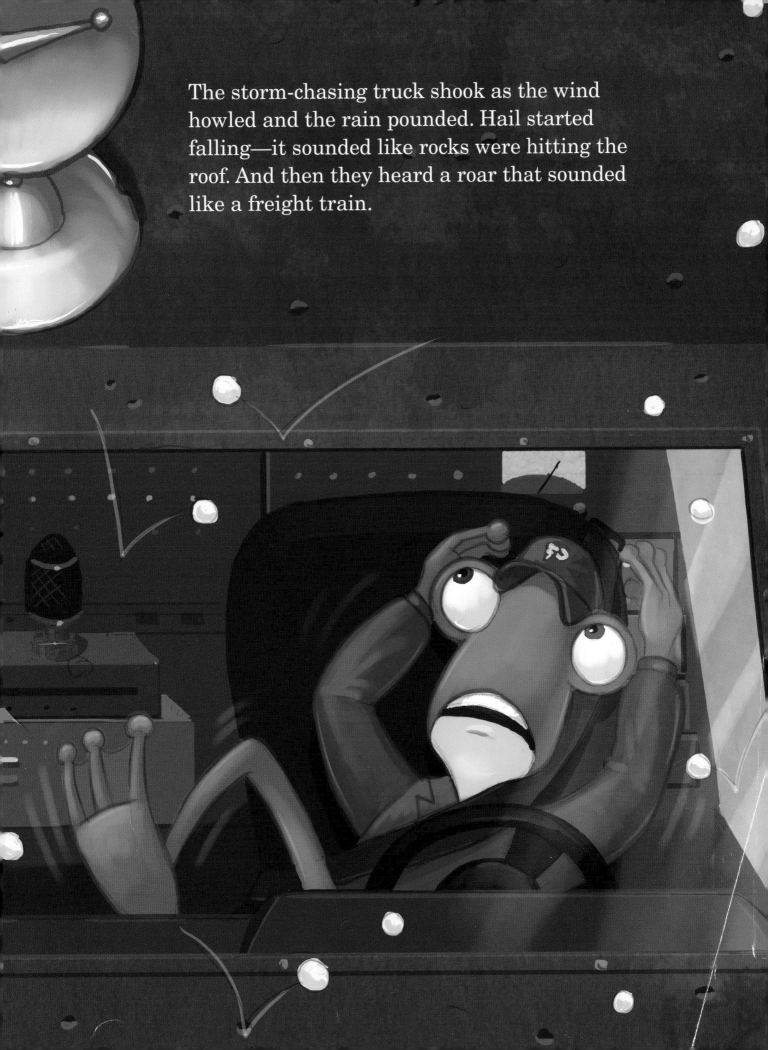

The storm-chasing truck shook as the wind howled and the rain pounded. Hail started falling—it sounded like rocks were hitting the roof. And then they heard a roar that sounded like a freight train.

Within a few minutes, the sirens stopped. The wind, hail, and rain calmed. The sky was clearing up, and it seemed the worst of it was over.

They drove a little farther and saw a lot of damage. The Tadmobile had been battered by falling tree branches and hailstones the size of golf balls.

"Holy croaks, folks! That was a close encounter with a tornado!" Tad said. "Look at the picture I took. That there is a wedge tornado."

Polly and Sally came running out. "You okay, Freddy? You look a little greener than usual," said Polly.

The police and firefrogs arrived, and the mayor stepped out of the fire truck. "You okay, Freddy?" he asked. "Thank you for warning us on the news! When we heard your report, Mrs. Mayor and I rushed down to our basement, where we were safe!"

"Weather can be very scary, Freddy," the mayor said. "But if everyone is prepared and knows what to do and where to go, it can save a frog's life. Thank you for keeping us safe. And Tad Polar, it's an honor to meet you. You are one great storm chaser."

Freddy called his parents to make sure they were okay. Thank goodness, they were. But unfortunately, Freddy's backyard weather station had been damaged by the storm.

The National Weather Service was out surveying the damage and determined an EF-1 tornado had blown through with estimated winds of 100 miles per hour. It was bad, but it could have been so much worse.

"Freddy, you can storm chase with me anytime!" Tad said.

"Thank you," Freddy said. "But I think I'll stick to reporting the weather from inside the Frog News Network."

"I'll leave the storm chasing to you."

Tad gave him a wink. "Let me know if you change your mind."

As Freddy hopped home, he gazed up at the beautiful sky. He couldn't wait to jump into bed and get some much-needed rest. Tomorrow he would start rebuilding his weather station with his dad—so that they would be prepared for the next storm. Because our friend Freddy is always weather-ready!

Hi, Frogcaster Friends!

What did you think of my latest tornado adventure? I have to admit, I was a little scared when Tad and I found ourselves a little too close to a twister. There are a lot of **storm chasers** who try to get close to storms for the purpose of observation or to learn more about how tornadoes form.

When people learn about storm chasing they think it's a cool job, but it can be very dangerous. Many storm chasers warn local police and emergency officials when a tornado is approaching, and some spotters help the National Weather Service record and report tornadoes on the ground. Those warnings can help save lives.

There are other storm chasers who put their lives in danger when they come too close to a storm. They can also risk the lives of others if they get in the way of emergency vehicles trying to save people. I always say we have to respect the weather and stay out of its way when it gets too dangerous!

What is a tornado?

As you saw in the book, a tornado is a funnel of rapidly rotating air that comes from a powerful, towering thunderstorm. Not just any thunderstorm, however; most of these tornado-producing thunderstorms are called **supercells**. Wind speeds of tornadoes can exceed 200 miles per hour, and the strongest ones can destroy large buildings, lift trees, and toss cars and trucks around like toys. On average the United States has 1,200 tornadoes per year.

Most tornadoes are on the ground 10 minutes or less—but in 1925 a tornado traveled 219 miles across Missouri, Illinois, and Indiana in 4 hours! (National Weather Service).

In 1924, a tornado that started in Aiken County, South Carolina, traveled 135 miles into Florence County! (National Weather Service).

There are certain weather ingredients needed to create a tornado. We are more likely to see tornadoes during the spring and fall when warm moist air from the Gulf of Mexico pushes into a colder air mass from Canada. Large thunderstorms often form when these air masses collide and a whirling, rotating funnel-shaped column of air can form inside these storms and connect with the ground. Once it reaches the ground, we call it a tornado.

There are many different types of tornadoes. The one we saw in the *Terrible Tornado* was a **"wedge" tornado**, but they come in all sorts of shapes and sizes.

Waterspouts are tornadoes that form over the water. Usually they are weaker than those on land. Waterspouts can sometimes move on shore causing damage and injuries.

Hail is created when small water droplets freeze in cold air in the atmosphere. These water droplets are lifted by big gusts of wind called updrafts and they freeze into ice. Once the ice droplets become heavy, they will start to fall as hail.

What is the largest hailstone recorded in the United States?

According to the National Weather Service, the largest hailstone was 8 inches in diameter and weighed about 2 pounds. It fell in Vivian, South Dakota, on July 23, 2010.

Where are tornadoes most likely to occur?

The geography of the central part of the United States, known as the Great Plains, has the perfect environment to bring all of the ingredients together to form tornadoes. This area is called Tornado Alley and includes Texas, Oklahoma, Kansas, Nebraska, Colorado, South Dakota, and Iowa.

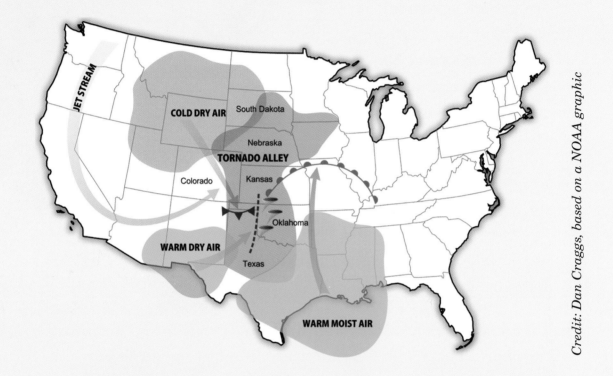

Credit: Dan Craggs, based on a NOAA graphic

What is the difference between a **Tornado WATCH** and a **Tornado WARNING**? (from NOAA)

A **Tornado WATCH** is issued by the **NOAA Storm Prediction Center** when there are weather conditions that are favorable for tornadoes. A watch can cover parts of a state or several states. Watch and prepare for severe weather and stay tuned to NOAA Weather Radio to know when warnings are issued.

A **Tornado WARNING** means a tornado has been reported by spotters or indicated by radar and there is a serious threat to life and property to those in the path of the tornado. If your area is under a warning, act immediately.

How do we measure the strength of tornadoes?

The most common way to determine the strength of a tornado is to look at the damage it caused. From the damage, we can estimate the wind speeds. The "Enhanced Fujita Scale" or EF-Scale was implemented by the National Weather Service in 2007 to rate tornadoes.

This EF-Scale grades the strength of a tornado. Two of the major factors are estimated wind speeds and destruction. It ranges from EF-0 to EF-5 (0 being the weakest and 5 the strongest).

Freddy's tips to know before and during a tornado:

BEFORE A TORNADO: Have an emergency plan. Make sure everyone knows the safest place to go. Prepare a kit with emergency food for your

EF RATING	WIND SPEEDS	EXPECTED DAMAGE
EF-0	65-85 mph	Minor
EF-1	86-110 mph	Moderate
EF-2	111-135 mph	Considerable
EF-3	136-165 mph	Severe
EF-4	166-200 mph	Extreme
EF-5	> 200 mph	Incredible

home. Have enough food and water for at least 3 days.

DURING A TORNADO: Go to a basement. If you do not have a basement, go to an interior room without windows on the lowest floor such as a bathroom or closet. If you can, get under a sturdy piece of furniture, like a table. If you live in a mobile home, get out. They offer little protection against tornadoes. Get out of automobiles. Do not try to outrun a tornado in your car. Instead, leave it immediately. If you're outside, go to a ditch or low-lying area and lie flat. Stay away from fallen power lines and stay out of damaged areas.

IF YOU ARE AT SCHOOL DURING A TORNADO: Every school should have a disaster plan and have frequent drills. Basements offer the best protection. Schools without basements should use interior rooms and hallways on the lowest floor away from windows. Crouch down on your knees and protect your head with your arms.

AFTER A TORNADO: Stay indoors until it is safe to come out. Check for injured or trapped people, without putting yourself in danger. Watch out for downed power lines. Use a flashlight to inspect your home.

For more information about tornadoes, visit NOAA's National Severe Storms Laboratory: www.nssl.noaa.gov/education/svrwx101/tornadoes.

Stay safe, friends!

Freddy the Frogcaster

Acknowledgments

To Roger Ailes, for the opportunity to work here at Fox and for your kindness and encouragement these last twelve years.

To Dianne Brandi for being a big supporter of Team Freddy from the very beginning.

To the brilliant Brandon Noriega who double-checks Freddy's meteorological accuracy.

To Debbie Burkhoff and Jill Whalen for helping me expand Freddy's webbed horizons.

To Dana Perino and Mary Stirewalt for suggesting Freddy should go on tour.

To Megyn Kelly for your friendship, and reminding me to keep reaching for the stars.

To Doug Brunt, Doug Hilderbrand, Jen Sprague, Yates, Yardley, Thatcher, Cole, Chase, Tripp, Anna, Kendall, and Warner for being my first readers and for your valuable feedback.

To Shannon Bream for being such a good friend and Freddy supporter.

To Russ Cox. You continue to amaze me with your talent. Freddy has never looked better!

To my support team at Regnery Kids—Cheryl Barnes, Marji Ross, Mark Bloomfield, Maria Ruhl, Emily Bruce, and Caitlyn Reuss.

To my mom Stella for always believing in me.

To my fellow meteorologists, teachers, and families who have read Freddy out loud in classrooms and at home across the country. I am so honored. I truly believe Freddy is inspiring our next generation of meteorologists and helping teach our kids how to stay safe.

To Sean, my love. The weather truly brought us together. If those waves weren't so high, our paths might never have crossed. I am grateful to those strong winds off the Pacific…

Enjoy more of Freddy's weather adventures in

978-1-62157-084-4   978-1-62157-254-1   978-1-62157-260-2